I CAN ONLY IMAGINE DAD

LEGACY OF AN UNKNOWN FATHER

by

FRANCES McHENRY

Edited by Frances McHenry

PAGE PUBLISHING, INC.
New York, NY

First originally published by Page Publishing, Inc. 2015

ISBN 978-1-68139-197-7 (pbk)
ISBN 978-1-68139-198-4 (digital)

Printed in the United States of America

Disclaimer

This book is a work of fiction. Names, characters, places, and incidents are products of the author's imagination or used fictitiously. Any resemblance to actual events, locals, or persons, living or dead is coincidental.

For bookings or orders
Contact Dr. Frances McHenry
(E-mail) frances.mchenry@yahoo.com

Book cover designed by:
Chari C. McHenry
Mock Design Group
832-202-9366
chari.mchenry@yahoo.com

Dedication

To God, for guiding my hands, mind, spirit, heart, and soul to responsibly tell the story and to pass a legacy on to my children and grandchildren.

CONTENTS

Acknowledgment

Many people have had an impact on my life and the birthing of this book. I would like to acknowledge a few of whom I am especially thankful to God for.

- My birth mother (now deceased) Bettye J. Smith, for her love of family, her sense of independence, boldness, and gift of hospitality.
- My stepfather (now deceased) Otis Smith, for his love and encouragement to complete my education and to not give up. A true father.
- My grandmother (now deceased) Mama Odessa Brossette—nurturer, spiritual mentor, for teaching me that all things are possible for those who have faith and that I should never let an obstacle hold me back.
- My grandfather Henry Brossette (now deceased), for loving me, protecting me, and letting me know I am special.
- Daughter Chari, thank you so much for encouraging me to complete this project, and thank you for always giving me your time, dedication, and resources. Daughter Francina, thanks for your encouragement.
- Aunts Eva Tilman, Amelia Brossette (both deceased), and Emma Lee Bankston—for their sense of style and grace.
- Sister Odessa Denise Smith, for your support and encouragement.
- Uncle Alvin Brossette Sr. (deceased), who stood in the gap as a father.
- Special teachers: Mrs. Marie Solomon (deceased), Mrs. Ellen Tademy Jerro (deceased), Mr. Walter Jerro (deceased), Mrs. Victoria Minor, Mr. Mackie Freeze, Mr. Richard D. Coutee (deceased), Dr. Harry Robinson (my former professor of English, children's literature at Muskegon County

Community College), Dr. Lewis Walker** (Emeritus professor of sociology at Western Michigan University) whose impact has lasted until present time, and Dr. Patricia Williams (professor of English at Texas Southern University) for exemplifying style, knowledge, and grace—a classy lady.

- Spiritual mentors: Sis. Ruth E. Gant (deceased), Sis. Lizzie Roberson, Elder Edward Roberson, Prophetess Clara Simon, Prophetess Dorothy Johnson (all deceased), Dr. E. D. Thornton, Prophet Nathaniel NWobu, Prophet Joseph Hargo.
- Drs. I. V. and Bridgett Hilliard, who taught me the Word and exemplified a spirit of excellence.
- Pastor Cassandra Scott of Turning Point Faith Ministries and Created 2 Produce—for sharing and serving as a midwife to my book,. You were the only one who cared enough to help me produce. I thought at the time. I was Created 2 Produce!
- Master Prophet E. Bernard Jordan and team: Chavda Golden—the first to prophesize to me about books.
- Ms. Merle Ray for being everything in this whole process: coach, encourager, editor.

CHAPTER 1

Are You My Father?

I have lived many years and have come to know a lot of people, but none as intriguing or powerful as those who knew my father. You see, I am in the fall of my life, and I still do not know who my real father is. No one has come forth to tell me. Those persons who could tell me are either dead or have refused to help me find the answer to this one simple quest for the truth. How cruel is it to live amongst people who keep secrets to protect their own lies?

It has been a lifelong quest of mine to find the answer to one simple question. I remember reading the fairy tale children's book *Are You My Mother?* by P. D. Eastman to my children. It tells the story of a baby bird who hatched and fell out of its mother's nest while the mother was out searching for food. I would cry secretly inside because I knew how that little bird must have felt. The young bird spent the first few days of its life walking around, asking everyone, "Are you my mother?" As a young girl, I yearned so badly for the love of a father. I would imagine myself walking around like that young bird, searching and asking everyone I came into contact with the age-old question that I am still asking today, "Are you my father?"

CHAPTER 2

I Can Only Imagine Dad

My mother, Jane, God rest her soul, is already dead and gone. From the little information she shared with me, she did the best she could do with the experience she had as a pregnant sixteen-year-old in the 1940s. Over the years, as she grew older, her story of who my father was remained the same—but physical features and other remarks made by her and others contradicted the facts she presented. Back then, young women who were found to be "with child" or "in family way" were shipped off to a distant relative quickly. Then when the child was born, they would return home, and the grandparents would raise both the daughter and the grandchild as their own.

Raised by my grandparents, I called my grandmother Mama and my grandfather Daddy. They were the only parents I knew, until one day, my grandfather came to see me at school. We lived right across the street from the school in Utopia, Louisiana. So he would drop in often and see how I was doing. He said that my "father" was home for a visit. All I knew of the man they called my father was that he was living out West.

The moment I laid eyes on him, there was never a connection. I knew this man could not be my father. He didn't look like me; I didn't look anything like him. But in silence, we stared each other down like gunslingers do in the old Westerns from television. It was as if he was thinking the same thing I was thinking, *You couldn't be mine.* After a few cold stares, he would pick me up in his arms and sit me on his lap. I was eight years old at that time. It was then that I began to entertain the thought that if this were my father, I could get to like this feeling.

The feeling of being adored, smiled at, and talked to as if I were important was something I did not have much as a child. So when this man came and showed me just a glance of affection, I took it. It became my weakness for him for many years, although he never fulfilled his role as a dad.

He was in my life and out of my life just as quickly as he came. Throughout the years, he would visit on scarce occasions: once when I was a teenager, and twice later after I married and had children. Each time in the later years, he would be more impressed with what I had than I was with what he had. We never bonded. On one occasion, he called and asked to borrow money, and on another, he called me again from out of state and asked if he could send his troubled teenage daughter from a another marriage to live with me and my husband's family.

Before I first met him, I used to lie in bed and wonder what he was doing and where he was. It was mind-boggling as a child to think that a parent could leave you and never look back—never wonder how you were doing and whether or not you were eating or well taken care of. I just couldn't bear the thought that my father didn't love me, so I held on to the little glimpses I got when this man was in town of what it was like to have a father in my life.

As I got older, my grandmother would share a great lesson to remember when reflecting on the man whom we thought was my father. In the fairy tale, the little bird ran into several animals during the search for its mother. Each time, she would get a reply something like, "No, silly, I'm a cat"; or "No, silly, I'm a hen"; or "No, silly, I'm a dog." Old folks used to say, "If it walks like a duck, quacks like a duck, and smells like a duck, then guess what…it's a duck!" Similarly, I learned that the statement works in the opposite manner. If it doesn't walk like a duck, doesn't quack like a duck, and doesn't smell like a duck, then guess what…it's not a duck! I could imagine myself walking up to this man and saying, "Are you my father?" And I would imagine hearing a reply back, "No, silly, I'm a…" *Anything but a father.*

So as the quest continues in finding my real dad, I decided to imagine him, what was he like, who was he with, and whether he even knew that I was his child. The thoughts of the other dad using me or, worse, rejecting me were too much to bear. So over the years, I just came up with my own story of who my dad might be.

My two beautiful now-grown daughters do not know who their grandfather is, and my grandchildren will never know their great grandpa. But this is the story I have of him in my imagination and in my spirit. This story has been fueled by the whispers I got at family reunions, the sneers and snide remarks I have grown up hearing from others, and secrets that have yet to be told from the rustic Louisiana bayous. Too often, I would get comments from townspeople. I would get words like, "As light as Frances," "you are lighter than both your parents," "you look just like..." Those words just served as a cruel reminder that I was not who I was purported to be.

As I grew older, I had opportunities to spend time with "the man" they called my father, but in those experiences, the certainty that "this man" is not my father grew in my spirit. I had comments and remarks about the identity of my father, but nothing that gave me a true connection to a firm possibility until....

The "until" was a beautiful day in spring when I was enjoying my time at a spiritual conference. I had made close acquaintances with wonderful women of God, and we spent our time together sharing history. On this particular day, all of these ladies were visiting in one of our hotel rooms in between the conference sessions. We were sharing our life stories, and I began to share my own story about the anguish and impact of not truly knowing who my father was. I spoke about "the man" they called my father, and one of the ladies who flowed in the prophetic said to me, "That wasn't your Pappy!"

She began to describe the man in details: his complexion, his hair texture, his posture, the color of clothing he liked to wear, and that there was some sort of gold chain hanging from his pants pockets. She closed by saying, "He is with you all of the time, just standing behind you."

I was dumbfounded by the information she gave me. All I could do was sit there motionlessly, staring into space as I pondered on this bombshell of information that had just been dropped on me. Everything around me seemed so surreal.

The wonder of who my father really is had always proven too great for me, but over the years, I learned to give the whole thing to God. Now to receive that spark that could lead to a revelation for me was quite heart stirring. My imagination is as vivid as the details initiated from the photos, remarks, and improper comments received from those whose hands I have suffered from all my life. It is at this point that I went into a trancelike state. All of the voices and people in the room I was sitting in all disappeared, and my imagination began to engage in a full vivid cinema flashing right before my eyes. The movie that plays is a time period from the past, and a story begins to unfold.

CHAPTER 3

Joe and Audrey

The year was 1919 in Aloha, a rural village settlement in Central Louisiana. Life was mundane and hard after World War I. On the other side of the old bumpy, dusty U.S. Highway 71, the only road at the time between Shreveport and Baton Rouge, there lived a widow named Audrey Franklin. She lived on Fletcher's landing with her brood of five children; they had arrived on Fletcher's West place to live among relatives as sharecroppers on Fletcher's plantation. Audrey was a demure woman with high cheek bones, which gave hint to the Indian heritage in her blood. Her hair was thick and wavy and hung like brown braided ropes which she had tied up in two braids that crisscrossed on the top of her head.

A woman in her forties, she was truly a beautiful woman to behold. There was a slight hunch in her back probably from scoliosis and hard work, but she could still turn the eye of any man both colored and white. She and her children settled in after an untimely death of her husband, Solomon, a hardworking man, whom Audrey fell in love with before the war. As sharecroppers, Audrey and the children now lived in a shack on the plantation picking cotton and farming. Luckily for Audrey, it was cotton-picking season and harvest time. She and her five children hoped to make enough money to move back to her hometown of Utopia and have a house built there of their very own.

News traveled fast in a small rural town, so the news reached Confeine Bayou five miles away of the arrival of the widow to Fletcher's ferry rather quickly. Joe Broussard had always had a roaming eye for the ladies; he was a classic ladies' man. A tall handsome mixed Frenchman with broad shoulders and curly thick black hair, any woman in the Louisiana bayous would be proud to be seen with him in his single days. Joe was curious to see what this widow looked like. He began to think of an excuse to get to meet this widow. So he packed up a burlap sack of freshly dug sweet potatoes and loaded them on his hitched wagon and journeyed across Highway 71 in search of this widow.

After several dusty miles, he pulled up on the Fletcher's place and inquired about this widow. Some nice people who lived in one of the neighboring shacks pointed toward the widow's place, figuring that Joe was sent by the owners to see that she got settled in. Joe made his way in front of her shack as Audrey's family was inside preparing for supper. Her youngest daughter, peering outside the old cracked shack window, yelled, "Mama, there's a man out there!" Audrey wiped her hands on her apron and followed her excited daughter to the garret.

By this time, Joe had unloaded the sack of potatoes onto the edge of the porch. When Audrey came into his presence, he immediately tipped his hat and retorted, "Good evening, ma'am. I hear you are new to Aloha, so I thought I would be neighborly and bring you over a mess of sweet potatoes for you and your young'uns. Name's Joe Broussard, and I live on Confeine Bayou there cross Highway 71."

"That's mighty nice of you. Happy to make your acquaintance, Mr. Joe. I'm Audrey Franklin," stated the widow Audrey extending her tiny hand.

He noticed the cotton fields had taken their toll on her hands as Joe held one of her hands and enclosed it into his unusually long fingers and palm. That was a trademark of the old Frenchman, Joe Broussard Senior, his father. As he held on to her hand a little longer, he became quite mesmerized by the beauty of this pleasant, seemingly shame-faced woman. There was something about her stature that was bold yet quiet. Her voice was soft as a whisper, but it spoke volumes to Joe. All the sounds of the area seemed to have hushed silence as Joe heard her speak to him for the first time. Magnetism and electricity were flowing from him at the same time. He found himself fighting to stand as he looked down into her deep brown calming eyes. The only thing that broke his trance was the sound coming from his restless horses in front of the wagon.

Audrey thanked Mr. Joe for the sweet potatoes, and Joe tipped his hat, turned quickly, and strolled back to his wagon to climb onto the seat. He felt he had to reach his seat quickly before he fell back on his heels, quite drunk from beholding her beauty.

Audrey thought to herself, *What a handsome stranger.* His dark as coal curly locks of hair shifted slightly in the evening wind as Joe looked down to her from his wagon. He bid Audrey farewell, "Bonsoir, madam," and called out to his horse, "Giddy up, Sally!"

On his ride back across Highway 71 to Confeine Bayou, Joe was preoccupied with thoughts of this widow. He arrived back home and continued his evening chores of slopping the hogs, milking the cows, and putting the horses in the barn. Joe was caught up in a world of Audrey. That evening at dinner, his mother, Philomene noticed that her son was distracted. Even though his beautiful wife Franny, who looked liked Pocahontas, had prepared an especially tasty dinner, Joe didn't seem interested in eating. Franny was an excellent cook and an even better housekeeper. Philomene observed Joe's actions, and she suspected he had set his lustful eyes upon this new widow. She knew her son had inherited his lust demons from his French father, Joe Senior.

That night, as Franny and Joe Junior retired for bed, Franny snuggled up to her husband, but he turned away and pretended to be too tired. Franny's feelings were hurt, and she pondered about what she may have done to repel him. Franny had no reason to question her attraction for she looked like an Indian princess herself. Her long dark silky hair hung to her waist, and her eyes were just as dark and exotic. She had a heavy bosom, very narrow waist, and broad hips. Franny was what was called a "real looker." Joe knew his wife was beautiful, but there was something that plagued him and caused him not to be satisfied with his wife alone. His roaming eyes continued to plague him.

The next morning, Joe arose very early. As he went about his morning chores, his thoughts were still on the widow Audrey. He was trying to think of another excuse to visit her again. As he worked around in the yard and pasture, he noticed the pear trees were laden with ripened pears, even the ground was covered with a complete sheet of yellow ripened Bartlett Pears. He fetched a bushel basket and began to fill the basket with succulent pears. Joe couldn't wait to see Audrey again. He didn't know what excuse he would use to get away from home that evening, but an opportunity did present itself.

Revival had started in Colfax, Louisiana, at Pilgrim Rest Baptist Church, and Joe knew his wife Franny would walk the two and a half miles to church with their children and some other neighbors who lived nearby. He knew they would leave early to reach the church in plenty of time before the service began. He would have plenty of time to go over on Fletcher's place and return home before Franny and the children returned! Bubbling inside with anticipation, he loaded the wagon with the basket of pears and covered them so he wouldn't have to waste any time making his hasty trek to Fletcher's place that evening. Satisfied with his plan, Joe calmly waited for the events of the day to play out.

Finally, evening arrived, and Franny summoned her family to dinner. She quickly fed them and started the bathing rituals in preparation for going to church. Joe quietly moved around the house watching Franny's every move. He paced himself to make counter moves for his trip across Highway 71 to see Audrey again. He even sat on the steps of the porch under the pretext that he was just cooling off before bathing, when in actuality, Joe sat there strategizing his movements with Audrey for the evening.

Franny and the children, Nathan and Geraldine, walked down the steps past Joe out the yard and down the dusty road toward the highway.

"Finally!" Joe whispered to himself. He jumped to his feet and quickly ran up the steps to get his bath. He bathed so quickly you could have sworn he threw the water up into mid-air and ran underneath it. He dried himself off and began to dress himself in his trademark style: starched ironed white shirt and black pants. Philomene inquired of her son Joe, where he was going in such a hurry.

"I think I'll take some of those pears for that new lady and her children since we got more than we can use."

Philomene lifted her brow in an inquiring manner. She knew Joe was up to his womanizing tricks again.

He rushed past his mother and hurried to the barn to hitch his horse and wagon, which was already loaded with the pears. He was on the buckboard in an instant and sped off down the dusty road toward Fletcher's landing. Joe really pushed his horse Sally. He kept hollering, "Giddy up Sally," while popping the reins repeatedly. There was a cloud of dust following his wagon like a foggy mist. Philomene watched in disgust until her son was clearly out of sight.

It wasn't long before Joe pulled up in front of widow Audrey's. As Joe climbed down from the wagon and Audrey's youngest daughter ran in the kitchen to announce, "Mama, that man is here again!"

Audrey came out to the porch and yelled, "Oh, Mr. Joe, good to see you again. How you doing this evening?" Audrey inquired.

"Just fine, Miss Audrey. Well, today as I was working around the farm, I noticed the pear tree was just loaded, so I thought I would bring you some because we have more than enough for us," stated Joe.

"Thanks, Mr. Joe. That's mighty nice of you!" exclaimed Audrey.

By this time, Joe had unloaded the pears and sat them on the porch.

"Mr. Joe, can I offer you a cup of coffee and a slice of sweet potato pie?" asked Audrey. "I took some of those sweet potatoes and made some pies last night," Audrey said.

"Speck I do, Miss Audrey. I have always had a sweet tooth," replied Joe.

"Well, have a seat, Mr. Joe while I fetch your coffee and pie," insisted Audrey.

As Joe sat there, mesmerized by Audrey's beauty, he didn't really focus much on the curious children that ran and darted about snickering and peering at this stranger in their midst. It was a scenario that had played out many times before as they moved from one little sawmill town to another.

Audrey soon returned to the porch with pie and coffee in hand. She bent over to hand Joe his coffee and pie, and her bosom was revealed to Joe. He savored every moment gazing down her bosom with the hunger of lust blazing in his eyes. Audrey startled him and brought him back to his senses as she said, "Mr. Joe, I sure hope you enjoy your pie and coffee."

"I'm sure I will, Miss Audrey," Joe sang out.

Audrey took a seat on the porch swing as Joe sat on the steps, eating away at his pie and sipping his coffee. She waited patiently while Joe ate, not bothering him with conversation. She was confident that she was a great cook, and Joe was enjoying her pie. She just propelled the swing with her tawny-colored shapely legs. Quiet as the wind with a soft breeze, she hummed. When Joe finished his pie, he exclaimed, "Miss Audrey, I 'speck that's the best piece of sweet potato pie I've ever tasted. Lady, you are a real cook!" he said.

Audrey replied, "Well, thank you, Mr. Joe. That's mighty nice of you! Would you care for another piece?"

"Don't mind if I do," he responded.

So Audrey lifted herself from the swing quickly and strutted over to Joe to replenish his saucer with pie.

Joe watched her with eyes of wonder as she walked off the porch back into the house. He was beginning to imagine what her tall and tanned body would feel like close to his. He was jerked back to reality when he had to pull out his pocketwatch from his pants to examine the time quickly. He knew he couldn't get his eyes too affixed too long on this lady; he would need to bid a hasty retreat back to his home before Franny and the kids could return from church. Upon checking the time, Joe saw he had just enough time left to sit and enjoy one more piece of pie in Audrey's company before having to return home. As he was putting his watch back, Audrey returned with a larger slice of pie than before. She handed it to him, and Mr. Joe took in every detail of Audrey as she leaned before him. Sitting quietly next to him on the steps as he devoured the second piece of pie, Audrey took in the crisp cool night air. The crickets chirped in harmony in the backdrop of the night, there was constant light flashing like Christmas lights from the lightning firefly bugs, and you could hear an occasional croak of a bullfrog on the bayou.

"Miss Audrey, how y'all coming along with your cotton picking?" asked Joe.

"Pretty good, Mr. Joe," Audrey began. "I heard Mr. Fletcher say we had already picked a couple of bales," she replied.

"That's good!" Joe said, pretending to care about work by carrying on conversation.

"Over on my side, we've not yet cleared that much. Well, when everything is harvested, the young'uns will be off to school. As soon as it gets a little cooler, I'll kill a couple of hogs, Miss Audrey, so I can salt and smoke us some meat for the winter. I'll be sure to save you a hind quarter," said Joe.

"Well, Miss Audrey, it's getting kinda late. I guess I'd better head back to the house Joe announced." Joe was tipped off by the sound of the Kansas City Southern freight train that traveled on the nearby railroad around 8:30 p.m. each night. The train was so regular that one could set their clocks by it. Heading north to Shreveport, the train carried freight from the New Orleans docks all the way to the interior states to Kansas City.

Joe handed Miss Audrey his cup and saucer and said, "Well, again, Miss Audrey, that was a mighty fine pie!"

"Good night, boys and girls," Joe extolled. And he tipped his hat to Audrey, the Southern gentleman that he was. He climbed up to his wagon, hating to leave the sight of Audrey, but he sat and disappeared into the night light and dust of the road as quickly as he came.

Joe pondered to himself, *What was it about this woman that had such an attraction on him?* It was like he was under a spell.

Soon he arrived back to his house and quickly unhitched the horse from the wagon. Joe made his way inside to undress and await the arrival of Franny and the children's return from church. His mother, Philomene called out, "Joe, is that you?"

"Yes, Ma, mere!" he replied.

"Joe, you are startin' to visit that widow a lot! What she looks like?" questioned his mother.

"Aww, you know, Ma mere. Just another woman," said Joe.

"Yeah, Joe, and I know you! Ma mere is going to give you a piece of my mind," said Philomene. "You play with fire, it will burn, Joe! You got a good wife, and no man could ask for a better-looking one! So stay your distance from that woman, Joe Junior, you hear me?"

"Yes, Ma mere!" replied Joe, but that warning was going in one ear and coming out the other one.

Joe had already decided that Audrey would become his next quest. Many women had caught his eye since he and Franny had been married some years, but none made his heart sink like the likes of widow Audrey Franklin.

Just then, Franny and the kids walked in from the night air, returning from revival. She was all ecstatic about the many sinners who had given their lives to Jesus that night. Franny spoke of how many were left on the mourner's bench with only a couple of nights left in the revival. Joe didn't hear a word; not only did he not share in Franny's enthusiasm, being a backslidden Catholic, his heart was set on this other woman. His mother, Philomene, listened to Franny as she talked without ceasing about the revival, and although Philomene was a devout Catholic herself, she thought she might try to go with Franny and the kids one night before the revival ended. Finally, everyone went to bed that night, and again, Joe gave Franny the cold shoulder.

At the crack of dawn, Joe's feet hit the floor with eagerness and anticipation for the day. As he began his chores, his mind was already on Audrey. He went about his farm work whistling, humming, and strategizing his next move so he could see her again. Not once did he think of his beautiful Franny as she worked diligently around the house. She washed, cooked, and cleaned, making everything in their old shack look neat, clean, and comfortable for Joe, his mother, and their two children. All the while, she kept purposely fixing herself up trying to show her husband that she was interested in getting his manly attention. But Joe had a one track mind: he was intent on getting something he did not deserve—the stolen love and attention of this other woman, Audrey Franklin.

Evening finally arrived, and Joe came in from the farm to a scrumptious hot dinner of fresh cabbage greens with spicy tomatoes and okra from the garden. Franny had cooked hot water cornbread to go along with the fresh vegetables and placed them on a plate that was ready awaiting her husband. Franny had always seen to it that her family's needs were met first, and then she and the children would be off about the house getting ready for church. Franny had been troubled by Joe's preoccupation, but she decided to keep the peace by blowing it off for the time being. Joe ate and stayed out of the way until Franny and the children were dressed and on their way. He then quickly got his bath and sat on the steps for a while so as not to stir up the watchful eye of his mother. But his restlessness got the best of him. He squirmed and stirred about trying to get the courage to tell his mother he was about to leave again.

"Ma mere, I think I will ride over to see a man about a hunting dog," he finally said.

His mother arched her brows, querying Joe about his goings. "Oh? Hunting dogs, tonight?" Without saying another word, Joe hurriedly got his horse, Sally, saddled and mounted, leaving as quickly as he could leave before Ma mere Philomene could say another word. He could not stand his mother's stares and questions.

As he rode Old Sally down the road, you could hear the gallop of Sally as she sashayed down the lane toward the highway. Heading across Highway 71, Joe stopped at Earl's place. Earl and his wife Georgette were relatives of the widow Joe had learned. He decided he would inquire of Earl if he had a hunting dog that he could get for a price. Georgette, Earl's wife, was Audrey's second cousin. Joe knocked and waited at the door as Earl and Georgette stepped outside and greeted him.

"How are your wife and family?" inquired Georgette.

"Oh, they fine, Miz Georgette. They gone to Colfax for the revival," Joe informed her.

"That's good, Mr. Joe. I have been planning to go one night myself, but I haven't made it yet. I'm thinking about asking Cousin Audrey if I can take her young'uns to the Raven Camp Fair and Pecan Festival on Friday night," Georgette informed him.

That was just what Joe wanted to hear—a chance he could visit Audrey without the peering eyes of her children. "That's just dandy!" Joe thought to himself.

"It's good seeing you, Mr. Joe. Let me get back in here and finish cooking dinner," Mrs. Georgette said as she nodded her head toward Joe. Mrs. Georgette was a tall woman like a Zulu or Ethiopian. She wasn't a pretty woman like her cousin, Audrey. Most folks would not look twice at her on the outside, but her sweet ways made up for her homely appearance. Joe wasn't quite sure if she was Audrey's cousin by blood, or if they just were friends that way because people back then called each other cousins whenever their families were really close to one another. Georgette was endowed with large breasts, and most of the Frenchmen, Cajun, white, and Indian men in this part of the Louisiana Bayous gaped lovingly at the sight of her buxom chest. She and Earl worked very hard as sharecroppers. They had not been blessed with children, so Georgette took to other relatives and friends children just as if they were her very own. That is why she wanted to visit Audrey that evening and ask for permission to take the children with her and Earl to Raven Camp.

Raven Camp was the place colored people held their fair each fall. Days were hot in Aloha, and mornings were chilly to downright cold; so were the evenings. At the annual fair, the weather was perfect for all sorts of activities children could get into at night, after they had worked so hard with their families in the fields during the daytime. The fair held all kinds of contests judging the best-looking and well-bred animals, the freshest and largest homegrown crops, baked goods with the best pies and cakes you ever tasted, and craft booths of all kinds. There was always plenty of lemonade, tea, cider, and sweet drinks, plus sandwiches made of pit-smoked meats for sale that had been cooked outside. You could smell the barbecue cooking over a pit of stacked bricks or over a discarded old ice box that had been turned into an outside oven. There were caramel apples, delicious pecans, miniature sweet potato pies, hotdogs, and popcorn balls— you name it! The children were more interested in the food stuff and games than the crops and livestock contests. Cousin Georgette knew that Audrey's children would really enjoy themselves. So as soon as she finished supper, she couldn't wait to walk down to Audrey's shack. Joe was all too happy to hop on the bandwagon, volunteering to walk over with her.

Although they all lived in dilapidated shacks, the ladies kept these broken-down old frame houses immaculate. The floors were scrubbed with lye soap that is considered poisonous and outlawed now, but back then, it made anything clean and as white as cotton. Beds were often covered with quilts that were made from colorful pieced together fabric creatively designed into some geometric pattern. Fall was also the season of quilting. A frame of wood would be setup in the sitting room usually, and the older women who couldn't work as much in the field anymore would work in the home and set aside time during the day to sit and sew on a quilt. Often it might be a collective community effort where the ladies would gather at one house and work together to complete a quilt. This group effort enabled them to complete a quilt quickly and to make each person as many as they needed for the winter. The women who worked in the fields would quilt at night by lamp light. They were so resourceful, using everything in their environment to provide for their families and their basic needs.

Audrey had taken what little she had and created as good of an environment for her children and herself as she could. Last night, after Mr. Joe dropped off the pears, Audrey and the children sat down and peeled the pears; Audrey slicing them. She took the pears and placed them in a large white enamel dishpan and spread them out evenly over the dishpan. Audrey covered the pears with sugar as she used to watch her grandmother do, so the pears could sit and soak all night in preparation for the canning process. As soon as she returned from the field that day, she made a fire and started the pears to boiling in order to make fresh pear preserves. Once the pears started to boil, Audrey made a large pan of her fluffy country white biscuits. Cousin Georgette had just given her some fresh churned butter that was whipped as light and fluffy as cream. So their supper tonight was going to be delicious—a simple meal of sugary sweet pear preserves, thanks to Mr. Joe. Those freshly baked golden brown biscuits, whipped butter, and a tin cup full of cold buttermilk for Audrey, and each of the kids to make their evening meal a marvelous treat!

The meal was finished cooking, and Audrey was fixing up the children's plates when one of the kids came running into the kitchen. "Mama, Mama, here come Cousin Georgette and that man again! They coming down the trail!" hollered the children.

Audrey was always happy to see visitors. Cousin Georgette and this handsome dark-haired, dark-eyed man made their way into the yard and up onto the dry-rotted creaking porch. "Audrey, what you doing in there?" yelled Cousin Georgette.

Audrey replied, "Hey there! Just in a minute, y'all take a seat. I'll be right out. I'm in the kitchen," yelled Audrey. Audrey emerged from the kitchen to the porch, "How y'all doing? Excuse me. I was fixing the children's plates and just putting them on the table. Why, Mr. Joe, how you doing this evening?" Audrey inquired.

"Just fine, Miss Audrey, just fine. I was just over to Georgette's talking to Earl, and when Georgette said she was coming to speak to you and the kids, I thought I'd walk over here with her," stated Joe. Joe's heart was pounding like a kettle drum as he laid eyes on Audrey.

"Please y'all have some supper with us," Audrey said as she wiped her apron, and the slight sweat from her beautiful fair-skinned brow. "I just cooked those pears you brought me, Mr. Joe, and I made a big pan of biscuits. We have plenty," she said. "Let me get y'all some," she said as she motioned toward the kitchen.

"No, no, Audrey. I just finished eating supper," said Georgette.

"Mr. Joe, I insist you taste some since you gave me the pears," commanded Audrey.

"Well, if you insist, Miss Audrey," Joe grinned.

"Now, y'all just have a seat and make yourselves comfortable," said Audrey. "I'll be right back when I bring Mr. Joe his plate. You kids come on to the table y'all plates are ready," Audrey beckoned to the children as they scurried to the table. The children sat contently, devouring those sweet pears and the fluffy hot biscuits while Audrey fixed Joe's plate and headed in his direction.

As Audrey approached Joe, his eyes were checking out every detail of her frame. As she bent to hand him his plate, once again he was feasting on her bosom. Joe's old lust demons were alive again. Not since he laid eyes on his wife had the hair on his chest started twitching like that. He did all he could do to contain his eyes to the plate instead of glassing them over Audrey's breasts, hair, and face. As Joe took his first bite, he exclaimed, "Oh, Miss Audrey, these biscuits so—as us Cajuns say—so good, they make you wanna shut the door! Lady, you can really cook!" shouted Joe.

"Ah shoot! Mr. Joe, don't tease me like that," said Audrey.

"No teasing, ma'am. I'm telling the god and heaven knows truth!" said Joe.

Just then, Cousin Georgette interjected, "Oh yes, Audrey can really cook now. She could always get a job in any white folks kitchen whenever she wanted."

Audrey sat down to talk with Georgette and Joe. After about an hour, and it was nearing sundown, Georgette decided it was time for her to return home. "By the way, Audrey, Earl, and I are going to the fair at Raven Camp tomorrow night. Have these children dressed to go with us. They need to get out and meet other children instead of just working the fields every day and going to bed. They'll enjoy themselves, and it will give you a little break too," explained Georgette.

"You know, that sounds just fine, Georgette. I'll have them ready!" Audrey responded.

Mr. Joe couldn't believe what he was hearing. An opportunity was presenting itself so soon for him to be alone with Audrey! He knew his wife, Franny, and the kids would be going to the final night of revival. Joe was so excited! He stuck his hands into his pocket and pulled out some change. He gave Miss Audrey coins for each one of her children. Audrey was so surprised by his act of generosity. "Oh no, Mr. Joe, I can't accept your money. What's this for? You already been too kind to me and my young'uns," exclaimed Audrey.

"Oh, I insist, Miss Audrey. Just a little something for the kids."

"That's mighty nice of you, Mr. Joe. All right, if you insist!" she exclaimed.

Cousin Georgette retorted, "Audrey, you don't have to be so proud to refuse help. You know you need all the help you can get with these children and then some."

"Well, thank you so kindly, Mr. Joe. Again, this is mighty kind of you," Audrey lilted.

"My pleasure, Miss Audrey. I just want to be of assistance in any way I can," said Joe.

Georgette stood up to leave, so Joe took the cue and said, "Miss Georgette, I'm gonna walk on back with you," Joe sang out.

"That's fine, Mr. Joe. Now, I won't have to walk by myself. Earl is probably sitting watching out for me," Georgette replied.

"Yes, and Ma mere's probably waiting for me too," replied Joe.

It was the beginning of the fall season, and the days were getting shorter and cooler compared to the long hot days of summer. At night, the bright full moon illuminated the sky. Georgette and Mr. Joe walked along the narrow grassy trails towards Georgette's house, and they soon saw Earl waiting on the porch for Georgette's return.

Joe yelled out to Earl, "Well, Earl, now that I've walked your wife back home, I'm gonna head on cross this highway toward home myself. Ma mere has probably been expecting me back anytime now. I'll see y'all later."

"Good night, Mr. Joe," Georgette said. "Thank you and good night!" Georgette and Earl replied in unison.

Joe strutted off into the moonlit night filled with excitement of his expected conquest the next day. As he walked along, he could hear an occasional howl of a fox in the distance. He also saw a raccoon and armadillo cross the road in front of him. Joe finally reached home and entered quietly as a mouse. He tried not to stir up any noise as he didn't want to face his mother's stern stares and verbal queries. Joe undressed quickly and got ready for bed; he smiled to himself thinking about the widow Audrey.

Soon after jumping into bed, Joe heard Franny and the children arriving back from church. After they all bedded down for the night, Joe could not fall asleep. He tossed and turned all night long with anticipation. Morning came, and he rose soon and went into the kitchen. As Joe made a pot of coffee, the smell of country roasted coffee beans filled the old shack, waking Franny and his mother. The two women arose from their bedrooms and entered the kitchen.

"Bonjour, Ma mere!" Joe extolled.

"Bonjour, Joe!" his mother replied, *"Comment ca va?"*

"Tre' bien, Ma mere," replied Joe.

"That coffee smells good, yeah!" bellowed Franny as she soon entered the room, greeting everyone with a beautiful "good morning, all!"

"Joe, you got coffee ready?" Franny inquired of her husband. "Why you up so early?" she continued.

"Oh, I guess I was just a lil restless this morning, so I decided to go ahead and get up," Joe lied.

Joe and Ma mere Philomene sat and drank coffee as Franny began to fix breakfast. She whipped out her pans for making biscuits from the cupboard and began to work her magic with the perfect blend of lard, flour, buttermilk, and baking powder into a round of perfectly light fluffy biscuits which she placed into the oven to bake. She sliced pieces of bacon from the slab and placed them into the skillet to fry. The room soon filled with the aroma of bacon frying. When the bacon was finished cooking, she broke those fresh brown chicken eggs into the grease left from the cooked bacon. Joe liked his eggs over-easy by just spooning that hot bacon grease over his eggs and then removing them from the skillet. Once on his plate, he would shake loads of black pepper over the eggs. Then he would break the yolks with his fork and take his biscuit and sop up the yellow yolks devouring them with pleasure. But this morning, Joe was having delightful thoughts of Audrey and him getting across Highway 71 tonight.

Soon, Joe, Franny, and Philomene finished their breakfast, and Joe left the house to embark upon his farm chores for the day. Throughout the whole day, he couldn't wait for the evening to arrive again. He had everything mapped out already.

On the other side of the highway, Audrey prepared breakfast for her crew before they headed out to the fields to work. She knew she had promised Cousin Georgette that the children could accompany her and Earl to the Parish Fair that evening. Her plan was to come in from the field early so she could have the children bathed and ready. She encouraged the children to be real productive since they had to cut short their picking for the day. All Audrey could think about was some time to herself; she craved a long leisurely bath. She planned to wash her hair to get rid of the sweat from working in the fields and to have a sip of that Muscadine wine she had made.

The children picked liked troopers. They were really eager to see what the rest of the community and its people looked liked outside of their world on Fletcher's farm. The hours seem to fly by like the speed of lightning, and before they knew it, it was time to head for their shack. Audrey had put on a big pot of beans to cook slowly while they were in the field working. By this time, the children were bursting with excitement. They were galloping, scampering, and giggling all over the place with anticipation as they formed a crooked line, making their way from the field. Audrey ordered the older children to go and draw water from the well for their baths. As they brought in the water, Audrey made a fire in the fireplace so the large kettle could be heated to provide hot water to mix for their baths. As the water heated, Audrey spooned up plates of beans and some leftover cornbread for them to eat. She didn't want to send her children away from home without them being fed, since their money was so sparse, and they did not have a lot of money to spend at the fair. She had the ten cents a piece that Mr. Joe had given the children and a few pennies that she could scrape together.

Soon, the children were supped and began taking their baths. The older children bathed first, reserving the water from their baths for their younger sisters and brothers. It wasn't a very sanitary practice, but that was the practical and economic way of their world. Audrey began to comb the girls' hair after they were dressed in their little flour sack dresses. When she finished the braiding of the girls' hair, she made the boys line up to have their hair brushed. If anyone of them resisted the combing or the brushing because it hurt, Audrey would cluck them in the head with the homemade boar's hair brush. After each one finished dressing, she made them sit down quietly on the porch until Cousin Georgette and Earl arrived to get them. They sat there as quiet as mice, anxiously waiting while Audrey stood in the doorway of the run down shack and gave them the laws they were to abide by for their behavior. She warned each one of them that if they misbehaved and gave Cousin Georgette any trouble, she would give them a good whipping and would not let them go anywhere else anymore. The children replied in unison, "Yes, ma'am!"

They immediately heard the hooves of a horse and the rickety screeching sound of the buckboard approaching. At that very moment, they spied the buckboard coming into sight and heading in their direction. Within a few minutes, Cousin Georgette and Earl were pulling up in front of their shack. Cousin Georgette shouted, "Hey, Audrey! Hey, boys and girls!"

Earl followed by replying, "How all y'all doing? Y'all ready to go?" yelled Earl. "Come on out here and let me help y'all into the wagon!" commanded Earl. He was so good with children. He had a gentle and kind way about him. He instructed the children to sit down on the floor of the wagon and to hold on the sides of the wagon. He climbed back up to the wagon quickly and took his seat gingerly beside Georgette, and they were on their way back on the dusty path they had traveled getting there and clear out of Audrey's sight.

The horse pulled the wagon up to the stop at U.S. Highway 71. Earl cooed, "Whoa, girl!"

As Earl stared up the highway for a moment, he yelled, "Giddy up, girl!"

They were now on their way southward toward Colfax. The children's eyes began to take in all that was around them. The bayous on each side of the road, the tall oak trees draped with hanging gray moss, pelicans diving into the water to scoop up a nice large fish for their supper, an occasional bullfrog croaking here and there, and a flock of buzzards feasting on some dead animal's carcass. Every now and then, they would spy an occasional weathered shack sitting back from the road. All they could hear was the constant gallops of the horse's hooves against the bumpy road. It was so good to venture out to see the countryside beyond their limited space and place.

Soon they were approaching an area called Rockhill. It was an elevated tall hilly area to the left as they were coming to the junction to go straight ahead to Alexandria or veer off to the right toward Colfax and Boyce. Earl took the road that went through Colfax. He wanted the children to see the town. As they veered off to the right and journeyed down the road, the children were in awe of the large mansions that were on each side of the road. The children wondered to themselves what it might look like inside the mansions. Each house was nestled under groves of pecan trees and to the back of these mansions ran a levee that protected the homes from the flooding of the Red River. Then the road took a sharp snake turn to the left and crossed over some railroad tracks and straightened out again as they began to approach the town. They were riding alongside the railroad tracks to their left that were coming into the town's railroad depot. The sign on the depot read Colfax. As they turned their heads to the right, they began to see store after store, right beside each other like a row of sitting ducks. The children were so excited to see the hustle and bustle of a lively town on a Friday evening, but they knew not to let out a sound because of the fear of their mother's warning still resonating in their heads.

Wagons lined the streets on each side, and people walked leisurely on the sidewalk from store to store, shopping for groceries and other supplies. Earl finally rode to the end of Main Street and turned right, and there in front of them, was the tallest building the children had ever seen. There stood the Grant Parish Court House as grand as grand could be. It was a short ride past the courthouse before the road turned again to the left. Now they were straight on their way to Raven Camp. Soon there were other wagons filled with colored families joining them on the road, forming a caravan heading to the fair. The caravan finally reached the turn off road to Raven Camp. The fairground was a large open area of field that was dotted with building, tents, and stands selling all kinds of food and drinks. The tents housed the animals and crops to be judged by the judges. There were gospel choirs competing for the best choir, sporting contest, and just plain old-fashioned fun. They finally arrived to the fair, and the children climbed down from the wagon and were a little bit shy at first, but other children came up to them and made friends with them. Soon they were off enjoying the fair and having the greatest time they had experienced in a while.

Back on Fletcher's place, Audrey had made herself a warm bath scented with rose water she made herself. Her tired body ached from all the field work, so she just wanted to sit and soak the tiredness away. As she sat in the water, she began to take down those criss-crossed braids and run her fingers through each braid until they were untangled completely. Her wavy black locks reached down her back into the water. She washed her hair to remove the sweat and dirt due to picking cotton in the fields. Audrey began to drift away in her thoughts of building that perfect house for herself and her children to live in. A house surrounded with all kinds of flowers. Although life had dealt her a bad hand, she was determined to get that house for herself and her children. After a while, the water in her bathtub had begun to turn cool and brought Audrey back to reality. She stirred her body to stand up and she stepped out of the tub. She dried herself quickly and put on the nice white gown her sister Amy had given her. Next, she towel-dried her wavy hair while, pouring herself a glass of that Muscadine wine. She put away the things from her bath away. Then she pulled up a rocking chair and sat in front of the fire hearth to relax and let her hair dry. Audrey was just sitting staring into the amber fire while sipping on that tasty wine. She was enjoying every minute of this quiet time alone.

Meanwhile across the highway, Joe was bathing and removing the stench of the workday from his body. Franny and the children had left on their way to the Revival. Joe grabbed that bar of lilac soap and soaped and scrubbed himself quickly. Excitement was at its peak now of him seeing Audrey. He stepped from the tub quickly and dried himself off. Joe grabbed the talcum powder and dusted himself all over, particularly his crotch. There was a white circle silhouette on the floor where he stood. He reached for his trademark white shirt and black pants and adorned the pants with his railroad watch and chain that was sitting on the dresser. Joe smelled as good as he looked. As he walked softly through the house, he grabbed a peppermint and placed it in his shirt pocket. His mom heard him and asked, "Joe, you going somewhere?"

"*Oui*, Ma mere! I'm going back over to Earl to see if he has gotten that hunting dog yet," he quickly retorted.

"Joe. I have warned you, so let your conscience be your guide," repeated his mother. Joe made haste and left the sound of his mother's scolding voice because those lust demons kicking up in him now had no conscience. Joe mounted his horse that he already had saddled and trotted off into the moonlight.

Audrey was relaxed from sipping that wine when she heard the sound of a galloping horse. *Reckon who can that be?* thought Audrey. Shortly, there was a knock on the porch. "Who is it?" inquired Audrey.

"It's me, Miss Audrey!" replied Joe.

"That you, Mr. Joe?" said Audrey, stunned at the sound of his voice behind the door.

"Yeah, it's me," Joe replied again. "Thought I would come sit a spell and keep you company since you over here all by yourself!" Joe tried explaining.

"Just a minute, Mr. Joe, let me make myself decent!" Audrey spoke as she went about searching for her coverings. Audrey grabbed a housecoat of sorts to cover her gown, and she dashed to the door. An alarm went off inside Audrey to not let this man into her shack, so she suggested they sit on the porch in the swing.

Joe had popped that peppermint into his mouth to refresh his breath. He lowered his body onto the swing, and Audrey slid into the swing beside him. Her hair was still down and somewhat damp. Joe took notice to her hair. "Oh, Miss Audrey, you look different with your hair down, you look simply beautiful!" Joe said as he adored her.

"Awe shoots, Mr. Joe, you must be kidding me," replied Audrey.

"No, Miss Audrey, I mean what I say," Joe stated innocently. They both began to propel the swing with their legs. Joe reached over and began to stroke her hair. "Your hair is so soft and silky!" Joe continued to stroke her hair.

"Mr. Joe, I don't think you should do that anymore," contested Audrey.

"Why not, Miss Audrey? I am just stroking your hair," Joe spoke softly but bluntly.

"It's a beautiful full moon tonight," Audrey emphasized, trying to turn the conversation.

"Yes, it sure is!" Mr. Joe purred. "Miss Audrey, do you want fifty cents to show to the moon?" Joe asked as he stood up abruptly and suggested Audrey stick her hand into his pocket and get whatever she wanted. Audrey complied reluctantly. Her hand fetched in his pocket searching for that fifty cents piece, but she made another discovery! Joe's nature was aroused! Audrey jerked her hand from his pocket abruptly, but before she could pull away her hand completely free from his pocket, he grabbed her hand and forcibly pulled her up from the swing onto her feet and into his body, and he held her tightly. Audrey took both of her hands and pushed herself loose from him. Joe apologized for his actions, extorting he didn't know what had gotten into him.

Audrey's thoughts were racing, thinking she needed to put some distance between them. She quickly thought about offering him some of that wine. "Mr. Joe, let me get you some of that Muscadine wine I made."

"Don't mind if I do," replied Joe.

Audrey rushed from the porch hurriedly and went into the house to get the wine. She was thinking by then why did she offer him wine instead of coffee? She stood in her kitchen somewhat shaken from his forwardness. Her hands shook as she attempted to pour up that glass of wine. Before she could return to the porch, Joe had tipped up behind her and grabbed her again. This time, his hold was tighter than before. He pressed his body against hers, and once again she could feel his arousal. He spun her around and began to kiss her passionately. His hands began to roam and explore sensual parts of her body. He was like a cat pouncing on a mouse. As his hands began to roam, Audrey lost all of her resistance. It had been so long since she had been pursued like this or touched this way. She knew it was wrong, but she gave in and lost all her resistance. Joe lifted her from her feet and began to carry her toward the bed he had spied out as he entered the room. He laid her onto the bed like a precious porcelain doll. At the same time, he was ridding himself of his shoes and clothing. He lifted Audrey's white gown and feasted on those breasts he had spied down her bosom. Joe was in perpetual motion now, nothing and no one could stop his actions now! He was completely enthralled into Audrey. All of these weeks of looking at Audrey and imagining had come to pass. Joe mounted Audrey as if he had mounted his horse Sally. But this was the new woman of conquest and not his horse. Joe was lost in Audrey's body. It was like fireworks on the Fourth of July. Joe wanted this encounter to last forever. He thrust and thrust away while whispering sweet words into her ears, and finally moaning while climaxing in ecstasy. Joe's body slumped on top of her, and he rolled off, still caressing her breasts. He was thinking to himself, Audrey was more satisfying than he had ever imagined—and then some! She was as good as her cooking! Audrey began to sob.

Joe turned over to her and asked what was the matter. "Mr. Joe, I shouldn't have done that! I never asked, but you are probably somebody's husband! Lord, what have I done? Please forgive me of my sin!" cried Audrey.

Joe grabbed Audrey and pulled her into his arms to console her. "There now, Miss Audrey, hush that crying! It is my fault, not yours," he stated. As Joe wiped the tears from her cheeks, his hands wondered down to her breasts again, and before Joe knew it, he was aroused again and laid Audrey down, and once again he mounted her, whispering, "There now, Audrey, my darling, don't cry!"

Joe took his time, savoring every thrust and deliberately holding back to prolong his enjoyment. Audrey thought this man was never going to be finished with her body. Old Joe sure had stamina. After what seemed like forever, Joe let out a loud moan, exclaiming, "Audrey! Audrey! Oh Audrey!"

He continued to lie on top of her, stroking her hair, nibbling her ear lobes, kissing her face, just lying there with his head on her breasts.

Joe lost all time and place. He seemed to forget about Confeine Bayou, Franny, and his children. His world was Audrey now! Audrey felt she was going to suffocate from the weight of Joe's body on top of her.

Suddenly they heard the blasting whistle of the 8:30 p.m. freight train as it headed north. Joe was jolted back to reality quickly. Joe rolled over to his side again, this time propping himself upon his elbow. Even though it was eight thirty, Joe knew he still had some time to linger before Franny would be returning home from church, and he would have to head home. He took Audrey's hand into his and began to kiss it. He knew he would have to leave soon, but everything within him wanted to stay here with Audrey.

At last, Joe decided it was time to leave finally. Audrey arose from the bed and followed Joe out of the house and onto the porch. When they reached the steps, Joe reached into his pocket and pulled out a fifty-cent piece and placed it in Audrey's hand and told her, "Don't forget to show it to the moon!" He kissed her good-bye and strode to his horse and climbed into the saddle. He tipped his hat and waved good-bye as he rode away slowly.

Audrey kept standing and watching until he was no longer in sight. She was experiencing flashbacks of her dead husband Solomon and feeling so remorseful about what had taken place between she and Joe.

Joe was almost home by now. He was pushing his horse to speed up now so he would have ample time to wash himself while out in the barn. Joe lit a lantern and found the towel and soap he had hid away and dipped them into the pail of water to clean himself up once he had returned that night. He wanted to stay out of sight and hearing distance from his mother. When he finished washing himself up, he entered the house and was surprised that Franny and the children were already home. Joe was so nervous! Franny asked him where he had been. He responded by saying he had gone over to Earl to check on that hunting dog!

"Oh, how is that Joe? We saw Earl and Georgette on the road to church," retorted Franny.

Joe began to stammer, "Oh yes, when I got there, they were not home so the neighbors told me, so I just sat a spell talking to their neighbors."

Franny knew Joe was lying, but she didn't press him any further. She also knew something was wrong by the way some women on the church ground were whispering and looking in her direction, giggling, but she didn't know what to make out of it. Franny just decided to be quiet and just watch Joe's actions.

After a while standing on the porch, staring and reflecting back on her dead husband Solomon, Audrey finally unclenched her hand with the fifty cents piece inside and displayed it to the brilliant full moon of the night. She whispered her secret wish and turned to hasten her way inside. She heated water again to take another bath and clean herself up before the children returned.

Soon, Georgette and Earl were knocking on the door to return the children. The children were so excited with all sorts of stories from the evening. Each one of them could not wait their turn to tell their story. Cousin Georgette gave Audrey a good report on the children. "Audrey, they were so well-behaved and had such a good time that I want to start taking them to Sunday school, if that's all right with you," uttered Georgette. "So have them ready Sunday morning around 8:00 a.m."

Each one of the children could not wait to take his or her turn telling everything they saw, heard, ate, and what friends they had made. The pangs of guilt continued to plague Audrey, but at the same time, she was so pleased that her children had enjoyed themselves so.

The rest of the weekend passed by quietly as Audrey started preparation for Sunday's dinner and getting the children's clothes ready on Saturday evening. On Sunday morning, all the children rose early, bursting with excitement about going to Sunday school. Audrey had them ready when Cousin Georgette and Earl arrived to get them. Audrey wasn't much of a churchgoer, but she liked to attend when there were singing quartets and usher board associations being held at one of the churches.

Franny and the children were dressed for church, and as they got ready to leave, Joe informed them that he was going to walk out to the main road with them. Deep inside, Franny prayed and longed for the time when he would walk all the way with them and attend services with her and the children.

They walked along briskly, and just as they came to the main road, there was Earl and Georgette pulling up to the road also. Franny took note of the other passengers in Earl's wagon. She commented inquiringly, "Whose children do Earl and Georgette have with them, I wonder? I reckon that's some of their kin."

Joe deliberately kept silent and did not respond to Franny's inquiry. Thoughts began to race in Joe's head, and he knew Audrey was alone again. Franny and the children started their trek toward the church, and Joe stood and watched them as they met up with some neighbors and journeyed on their way until all were clearly out of sight. Then Joe made haste across the road toward Audrey's place quickly. Audrey had decided to take her another one of those leisurely baths. She had immersed herself into the tub when Joe arrived. Joe rapped on the porch lightly, but Audrey did not hear him or respond to him. He decided to walk to the door and knock again, but there was a crack between the ill-fitting door. As he peered inside, he could see Audrey was in the tub. Joe was so aroused at this point he took his pocket knife from his pocket and lifted the latch from the door and let himself in.

Audrey was startled by his presence. "Mr. Joe, how did you get in here?" Audrey lifted herself frantically from the tub and was desperately trying to find something to cover her nakedness. Joe spotted the towel she was going to dry herself with, and he stepped forward to get it. He held it out in his hands as a father would beckon a young child to walk in his direction and walk into his arms to be dried off. Audrey didn't comply at first, as she continued to search for anything within her reach to cover herself with. She could not find anything large enough to cover herself, so after much spent effort on her part, she slowly and reticently walked into Joe's arms. He didn't pounce on her right away, instead he took the towel and wrapped it about her. Those long fingers began to stroke her body with the towel. In the full light of the day, he began to inventory and savor each part of her entire body. He began to stroke her breasts and downward toward her private parts. Joe was in deep heat now. His crotch was on fire!

Audrey began to yell, "No, Mr. Joe!"

But Joe was going for the kill now. He knew just the spots to touch and caress to get Audrey to lower her inhibitions. This time, they did not make it to the bed. Joe lifted her unto the table and mounted her there in the heat of his passion. Joe began to cry out Audrey's name. "My darling Audrey, you make me do things I don't mean to do!"

Joe continued to have his way with Audrey that day, and she became his Sunday play toy.

As time went by, Audrey arose one morning to fix breakfast for her children, but as she got out of bed, she became dizzy. She knew she could not afford to get sick, so she brushed it off and proceeded to make breakfast. But as she fried the bacon and eggs, the smell from these foods made her so nauseated that she had to make a mad dash to the back door of the shack where she vomited violently. Despair hit her in the pit of her stomach. She knew these symptoms very well because she had experienced them many times before, coupled with the fact that her menses were late. She leaned against the door frame and began to wonder to herself what she was going to do! Her oldest daughter Freda called out to her, "Mama, you sick?"

Audrey scowled, "No, Freda! Fix y'all's plates and feed your brothers and sisters!"

As Sunday rolled around, Joe came for his usual visit, but Audrey did not greet him in her usual cheerful way, and Joe sensed something was wrong. She was all sad and distanced in her thoughts. Joe began to stroke her hair, and she pulled away and began to cry. Joe pulled her to him again and held her. He asked her what the matter was. She burst forth in tears that she was in family way! Joe was silent for a while, as a deluge of tears continued to fall from Audrey's eyes. Joe finally spoke and said, "My darling Audrey, you know I'll do right by you! Stop your crying, woman. That's my baby, and I'll take care of my baby and you!"

Joe was a man of his word, and he began to bring provisions and leave them on Audrey's porch. Sometimes it might be a mess of greens, a smoked ham, and some bacon, some pecans, a side of beef, sugar, flour, cane syrup, milk, butter, eggs, potatoes, and anything else Joe felt would help Audrey and her children.

Months passed, and Audrey's belly grew with child. Joe continued his steal-away visits. On one occasion, Audrey had him feel her stomach. Joe was happy as well, but there was a fear in him of what

Franny might do if she found out! As Audrey began to show, gossip began to spread about her situation. Speculations began to circulate about who had been hanging around her and who the father was.

Well, as you might imagine, news spread so quickly that Franny got word of the situation. She was hurt deeply and was planning to leave Joe, but she needed to make plans to leave. In the meantime, she kept her composure waiting for an opportunity to confront Joe. So on that coming Sunday, Franny and the kids left for church—or so Joe thought. When he thought they were well on their way, Joe made his usual trek across Highway 71 to Fletcher's place to see Audrey. In the meantime, Franny had the children walk on to church with the neighbors, and at first, she started back home. But in a few steps more, she crossed the highway instead and headed to search out this woman Audrey's shack.

In the meantime, Audrey and Joe were in bed, and Joe was about to sip some of that Muscadine wine, when there was a knock outside. Audrey got up and walked to the porch, and there stood Franny. Each woman was sizing up the other.

Audrey thought to herself, *His wife is so beautiful, why would he want me?*

Franny thought, *I don't see anything so special about her that he would cheat on me like that.*

Each woman came to the realization that Joe was a *whoremonger*! That each of them had been betrayed by Joe! Franny stopped her staring and composed herself and asked in a firm voice, "Joe in there? Tell him to come out!"

By that time, Franny pulled a pistol from her purse and was standing with her arm folded down, holding the pistol with one hand pointed under her armpit. Joe put on his clothes hurriedly and made haste to the porch. As he walked toward Franny and down the steps, he spotted that shiny pistol in her hand. He knew Franny was a sweet woman, but she was not one to be riled. That Indian blood would get stirred up in her, and she was not one to be messed with, and he was even more afraid of those mean brothers of hers.

She shouted, "Joe Broussard, get in front of me and get to stepping!"

Joe was more afraid of what Franny might do with that pistol than his affection for Audrey. So he complied with her command and began to step briskly toward their house. Franny didn't argue or say anything at the time. She just followed behind him, stomping! They finally reached home, and Ma mere Philomene was surprised to see them arriving together.

"Franny, what are you doing home so early, and where are the children?" Ma mere asked, puzzled.

Franny let it out angrily. "I just caught your son over to that woman's house, and she is in family way with Joe's child! So I am packing and leaving Joe!" screamed Franny.

"Franny, please don't leave and take my grandchildren away from me! Please think about this!" Ma mere pleaded. "Joe, what have you gone and got yourself into? I warned you about playing with fire!" Ma mere hollered. "Now, if Franny leaves you, I don't blame her! You just like your father!" Ma mere yelled with tears in her old eyes.

Franny left their presence and headed speedily into their bedroom and began to throw clothes onto the bed. She was searching frantically, trying to find something to pack her things in. She found a couple of flour sacks and began to stuff clothing into them. She packed just enough to leave and threw the sack across her back like a hobo's sack, and she stormed out the house, walking hurriedly to leave this place. Joe followed after her pleading for her not to leave! But Franny kept stepping almost running, trying to escape this place and the man that had caused her so much pain and heartache. Franny really didn't know where she was going, but she knew some of her kin would take her and the children in.

As Franny walked, she stumbled along, blinded by the tears that poured like a waterfall from her eyes. She questioned herself about her looks. *What did this woman have that she didn't have?* She knew she had been a good wife and kept an immaculate house. What more could a man ask from a woman? Why would he want this widow with all those children that weren't even his? Franny's mind was being bombarded with all kinds of thoughts. She picked up her pace, just wanting to put more and more distance between herself, this place, and Joe. She finally reached Colfax and headed to one of her brother's house. His name was Joe also. Everyone was afraid of him, whites and coloreds alike. No one messed with Mean Joe Nesbitt! So when Franny arrived and told Mean Joe what had happened, Mean Joe

Nesbitt was ready to go on the warpath and pay old Joe Broussard a visit! Franny pleaded with her brother not to go after Joe! She told her brother that she needed to go up to Pilgrim Rest Church and fetch the children. So her brother calmed down for now, and he walked with Franny to the church to get her children.

The children were surprised to see their mother arrive with their Uncle Joe. Franny told them they were not going home now and that they were going to spend some time with their Uncle Joe. The children were confused and began to question their mom as to why they were not going home today. She told them Uncle Joe needed her to stay and help him out for a while. Everyone knew that Uncle Joe was so mean that he could not keep a wife himself! The children accepted their mother's explanation with much reservation. In the meantime, Uncle Joe pretended to be calm, but inside he was planning his attack for his brother-in-law Joe Junior. He knew opportunity was going to present itself to him sooner or later!

Franny and the children settled in with her brother Joe, and the children began to enjoy being in town, but back on Confeine Bayou, Ma mere missed Franny and the children. Ma mere found herself weeping for their return. Joe found his mother weeping, and he could not stand for her to cry. He asked his mother, "Why are you crying like that?"

She broke down in her son's presence and confessed she was hurting—hurting behind all the memories she had of going through that same pain with his father. She told her son that the only thing she had now was him, Franny, and her grandchildren; and she did not want them to destroy their love for family like his dad had done because of women! She explained to Joe Junior that even though his father was dead and gone, the pain of that kind of betrayal never goes away. Ma mere further broke down, crying even more bitterly, stating to Joe that she wanted her grandchildren and her family back!

News had reached Audrey's four sisters about her condition and the breakup of Joe and his wife. Her sisters knew the reputation of Franny's brother, Mean Joe, and they knew he was going to take revenge for his sister. So they all—Mary, Bertha, Amy, and Nora—decided they were going to go and move their sister off Fletcher's place and back to Utopia, to their home. Several of the sisters were old maids and had never been married, so they decided to give Audrey a place to live with them. Led by Bertha, the most outspoken of the four, the sisters put a plan of action together speedily and soon arrived at Audrey's shack to move her and her children. The sisters arrived in two wagons, along with some of their pistol-packing, muscle-bound mean cousins. Audrey hated to move, but she knew it was best for everyone. She did not want any more trouble on her part, and surely did not mean to cause Joe's wife any heartache because she had once been a wife herself. Audrey only had a few belongings, so it did not take long for them to have the wagons loaded and on their way. The children were glad to leave this place and live with their aunts, who had nicer houses to live in.

Audrey settled in among her sisters. Her children often slept in one place and spent the day at another one's house to be babysat or nursed. When they were all settled in the new place, the school-age children finally got enrolled in school. They loved being in school and learning to read, write, and count. Most of the children at school were their relatives anyway. This was so much better for the children instead of being on Fletcher's place!

CHAPTER 4

The Baby

Several months passed, and Audrey soon gave birth to the baby. It was a beautiful boy—almost the spitting image of his father. The baby was calm and easygoing like Audrey; she named him James. Everybody in the family was so happy and excited about the news of the baby. They all rushed right over to see him. But Mary, Amy, and Nora—the childless sisters—made the biggest fuss over him as he was welcomed by those aunts.

Joe managed to keep up with what was happening with Audrey. He continued to send provisions for them. Immediately after the baby was born, Joe made a surprise visit to see it. He was so happy to see Audrey again too. He expressed his joy about the baby.

Audrey's sisters were not happy about Joe's visit. They expressed their displeasure by saying, "He won't get the chance to drop off another baby here!"

When Joe left there, he decided to go through town. He walked down a side alleyway into the colored beer tavern, and there stood his wife's brother, the in-law, Mean Joe, who already had his fill of beer. As soon as Mean Joe spotted him, he lunged at Joe Junior. The two men tied up and wrestled about on the floor. Mean Joe was trying to get his pocket knife out of his pocket, and Joe Broussard held on to Mean Joe's arm, trying desperately to force Mean Joe to keep his hand in his pocket. They rolled about on the floor what seemed liked hours when Sheriff Thompson walked in and fired a shot in the air, ordering them to stop. Someone grabbed Mean Joe and pulled him away as someone else did the same for Joe Junior. Mean Joe was trembling with anger, brandishing his knife as he shouted over to Joe Junior, "This ain't over. I'll make you sh_t on my wrist!"

The sheriff did not arrest them, but he threatened them, and told each one to go home. Since both Joes had to go home in the same direction, Joe Junior was told to leave first, and Mean Joe was held over to give Joe Junior a head start.

As if that weren't enough, Audrey's cruel cousins were there in town too, and they did not like Joe Junior either. If the sheriff had not come, they were hoping Mean Joe would do the job of getting rid of Audrey's problem for them. The cousins Jesse and Eugene came to Mean Joe's aid. They figured the opportunity they all wished for would probably present itself again, and they would be ready next time!

Joe Junior realized he had narrowly escaped death at the hand of Mean Joe, and he saw the alliance that had formed between Audrey's folks and Mean Joe. He knew it was not safe to go hanging around Audrey anymore. With so much hanging in the balance, Joe had come back to his senses really fast!

Ma mere heard about the ruckus between Joe Junior and Mean Joe. She really gave him a verbal lashing. "I warned you, Joe Junior! You going to get yourself killed over that widow! Leave that woman alone! You better go and get Franny and my grand-bebes back! I want you to fix this mess you got us all upset about. You hear me?" Ma mere retorted.

The next day, Ma mere hitched the wagon and left without any explanation as to where she was going. The loneliness of missing her grandbabies had become too much for her to bear, and the fact that her only son was almost killed by Mean Joe was sending her on a mission today. Ma mere pulled up to the general store and went inside to buy her some snuff and her favorite peppermint candy. Then she headed on to see Franny at Mean Joe's place. Franny was out in the backyard doing laundry. She had begun to do white folks' laundry to earn money to help herself and the children. Franny was so happy to see Ma mere. The two of them hugged and greeted each other. The children soon appeared and made a mad dash into their grandmother's arms.

"My bebes, Granny has missed y'all's so much!"

She held them for what seemed like forever. She did not want to let them go for fear; she would not see them again. She finally let them go, and she handed each one a peppermint. "Now y'all go play, while Ma mere talk to your mother," commanded Ma mere.

Ma mere Philomene began to give Franny motherly advice. She loved Franny like a daughter. She began her appeal by telling Franny that Joe was her son, and she knew he was not perfect but then, who is?

"I know you love him, and he hurt you badly! Tell me what woman that has not been disappointed by a man? Franny, can you find it in your Christian heart to forgive Joe? I know Joe loves you and the children. He has been lost since you left. So come back to your home with me today! Your children love and need their father. Do it for me, if not for Joe. You know I'm getting up in age, and my family means everything to me. Life on Confeine Bayou is not life anymore. It's just plain sad around there. Joe busies himself, but I know he misses you all. He's just plain too stubborn and proud to admit it. That woman is gone on about her business with her folks, and I don't think Joe's going to be messing around her now! So, my daughter, come home to your husband! You not the first woman to be hurt, and you won't be the last," Ma mere spoke to her kindly.

"Men are just little boys, parading in men's breeches!" she said. "Get your things together whiles I talk to your brother," completed Ma mere.

"Howdy, Mr. Joe, how you doing?" said Ma mere to Mean Joe. "I come to get Franny and the children. I know my son was wrong, and he's payin' for his mistake. He gonna be payin' in heartbreak for a long time. Meantime, I don't want any harm to come to him. He's my only son and whoever tries to harm Joe Junior, they going to have to answer to me. I don't speck Louisiana is large enough for them to hide and get away from me! So just me and you stay out of their business and let the Lord have his way, Mr. Joe. That's all I ask you," stated Ma mere. She was a proud but wise old woman. She could stand up to any man. "So good day to you, Mr. Joe. Nice visiting with you!" said Ma mere Philomene as she took a big hark and let out a wallop of snuff spit as if to draw the line and mark off her territory to double dog dare Mean Joe to cross it!

Franny returned to her home as a result of Ma mere's persuasion. She had a love-hate feeling for this place now and for her husband, Joe. Once they arrived home, the children sped out to the field to find their father, whom they had missed so much. When Joe looked up and saw his children approaching, he threw down the hoe he was working with and started running toward his children with open arms. They finally reached their father, and they collapsed in his arms. He picked them up one at a time and tossed them in the air, only for them to return to his arms. Tears began to form in Joe's eyes. He thought to himself, *How I have hurt them and what a mess I have made of our lives!*

"How did you get here?" Joe asked the children.

"Ma mere came and got us!"

"Is your mama here too?" Joe said with uncertainty in his voice.

"Yes, Papa. Mama is in the house with Ma mere!" Joe began to walk toward the house with the children in tow.

Franny was in their bedroom, putting her things away when she sensed Joe's presence. As she turned, he didn't give her a chance to speak; he just grabbed her and held her for the longest time. Joe wept like a baby and fell on his knees, asking Franny to forgive him! There was sincere remorse in his voice. He really didn't know what had gotten into him or why he acted like that. He just knew he had always had that problem with a wandering eye for other women, but this was the first time he had ever taken it this far.

Franny just replied, "I know, Joe, I know!" Franny truly loved her husband, but the bond of trust was broken, and she just didn't feel the same toward him. As time went by and they returned to their daily routine of life on the farm, Franny went about doing her daily chores and talking to God a lot throughout the day, asking Him to mend her broken heart and help her to forgive her husband.

Joe finally confessed to her that he had been plagued by what he had done, and he was constantly thinking about the child he had fathered; he told Franny he wanted him to know his father. He confessed that he wanted him to be a part of their family and that he felt like he should provide for him rightly. Franny just stared at him! She was just plain numb, and she didn't know whether to stand there and continue to listen, or just start running until she was far away from Joe.

All of this news was just too much for Franny to take in at this moment. She just walked from the room and started walking toward the field. She walked for what seemed like forever when she came to a huge tree stump and sat down on it. She began to pray like she had never prayed before. After a while, a peace came over her like she had never experienced before and a still quiet voice resonated within her to "forgive!" Franny was a very religious woman, and she had deep compassion for her fellow man. She knew that baby was just a little innocent child and that she could not hold anything against it. But she needed more time to heal and get used to the idea that Joe had an outside child.

The baby was weeks older now, and Audrey went to work for the Hartman's. They were the town's bankers, merchants, and land barons. They had merchant shops, cattle, and a lot of land. Audrey's elder sister kept the baby while she worked. She cooked and cleaned for Mr. Bob Hartman, and her sister, Mary, did the laundry for them. Each time Audrey got paid, she would put aside as much as she possibly could for the house she wanted to build for herself and her children.

Bob Hartman's neighbor was Mr. Ed Miles, the town's surveyor and carpenter. Mr. Miles would watch Audrey each day as she would walk to and from work. The old Audrey charm was at work again. Audrey was lucky that she didn't have to buy any land for her house. Her father, Caesar Johnson, had already purchased acres of land from the Hartmans, and each one of his daughters could pick a piece of his land to build their own house on. Audrey decided to speak to Mr. Miles about building her a house.

Mr. Miles was already smitten with Audrey, so he eagerly volunteered his time as long as she bought her own lumber. She soon had enough money to build the foundation. Little by little, Mr. Miles built Audrey the house of her dreams. Mr. Miles was a great artisan, and he had spared none of his artistry on Audrey's house. It wasn't long before she had one of the grandest houses in town, among both coloreds and whites, with the exception being the Hartmans' house. Audrey surrounded her home with the most colorful flowers. You could pass by anytime and see her working in her yard. Although she was a quiet, demure woman of very few spoken words, her reputation had exceeded her. People had come to know her as the quiet widow who could turn heads and get things done.

When it came time for the baby to come to his home, Joe could not get it off of his mind. He had thought about him ever since he was born. He held both a sense of responsibility and love for fathering him, even though he had children already in his marriage to Franny. Since the child was now weaned, he was an old enough boy to leave his mother to be reared by his father. It was the first time Joe had ever prayed to God for anything. He asked God to please help Franny bring him into their home to be raised by him along with his older children. Joe felt so bad by what he had done to Franny, Audrey, and his children. He was now developing the heart of a real father, and he wanted to give his child a home. Joe felt he could not have if he continued to live with Audrey as a widow with five other children. Franny, though heartbroken over Joe's adultery, had a loving heart; she was not just a churchgoing woman. She really believed in the Word of God. She humbly agreed to allow Joe to raise his son in their home and to treat him as he was her own. Audrey didn't object very much to Joe's request because she still had five other children to care for, and besides she was working every day. So the boy was sent to live with his father. As he became school-age, it was decided that he would attend school in Utopia where his mother Audrey lived, but return to his father house each day. Several of Audrey's cousins were teachers themselves, so Audrey's children were taught and mentored by their cousins.

Whenever the Hartmans would discard some books, Audrey would retrieve them and bring them home for her children to read. Audrey had such a determination for her children to be educated properly, particularly the girls. She felt the girls could marry well if they were educated, and the boys could get a job working at a saw mill or in the fields. She wanted better for her daughters than what she had to endure at the mercy of men for her to survive.

As time passed, James grew into a young boy. As a young boy, James was easygoing like his mother, Audrey. He was quiet and observant of everything around him. He used to sit and reflect on things many days after helping Joe work in the fields. Not just a good farm hand, James was a quick learner and a humble young boy. He followed his father around everywhere his father went.

CHAPTER 5

How My Mother Met Him

Years passed by, and James was quickly turning into a young man. Joe had taught him to farm and had provided a wonderful home environment for him to be reared. James was an independent thinker, and when he got older, he decided to return to live with his mother, Audrey, and his siblings. There had always been a distant and coldness between James and his stepmother Franny.

After all, the fallout between the two families during the affair between her and Joe, Audrey thought it best to move away from Fletcher's landing, putting distance between herself and Joe. She moved back to her home town in Utopia and settled in the house built by Mr. Miles, living next door to her sister, Bertha, who had always been protective of her. Bertha was the one who had gotten the other sisters together and moved Audrey off Fletcher's landing. It was her idea to bring the mean cousins along just in case Joe or anybody else had something to say or stood in their way. Bertha had gotten her shrewd ways from their father, and she was always in her siblings business trying to run their households. Audrey became quite comfortable as a widow surrounded by Bertha and her other three sisters. All Audrey wanted now was for her daughters to become finely educated so they could become grand pickings to be married off into reputable families. Because Joe had reared James, Audrey didn't seem much concerned about him as a young man moving back home to live with her again. While she and Bertha were focused on rearing their girls into fine upstanding women to be married off. James, now a young man, was setting his sight on the new world around him.

Bertha's youngest daughter, Martha, had a best friend named Jane. They would visit each other's house nearly every day. While Audrey, Bertha, and even Jane's mother, Ruth, were busy trying to get their older daughters who had finished school married off into decent families, the younger girls, Martha and Jane had lots of opportunity to get into mischief together. Jane was a natural leader who never met a stranger. She was very comical and would have everyone laughing with her antics and humor. Martha, on the other hand, was a perfect host and would always provide plenty of Southern charm and hospitality for them as they explored things to get into around the house.

One day in the spring, as Martha and Jane roamed about Audrey's lush flower garden playing and telling jokes, Jane spotted a handsome young man sitting on Audrey's porch. Jane began to snicker and grin. "Who is that good-looking fellow with the dark curly hair and deep eyes?" Jane inquired.

Martha replied, "Oh, that's just Cousin James, Aunt Audrey's son. Come on, I'll introduce you to him." Martha insisted.

The girls moved toward the house continuing to giggle and frolic about, eventually opening the garden gate and entering the yard. They strode up the concrete walkway to the steps onto the porch. Jane wasn't the least bit shy as she approached the handsome stranger. "Cousin James, I want you to meet my best friend Jane!" announced Martha.

"Hello Jane," James responded. "Hi, how are you? Nice to make your acquaintance," he continued.

Jane responded giddily, "Hi, nice to meet you!" She was shifting her weight from side to side while crossing her feet and stumbling about, even though she wasn't usually the least bit shy. James didn't pay much attention to them; he simply smiled and went about his way, disregarding them as two silly young pretty girls.

Each day, Jane returned to visit Martha as was her custom, so she could catch a glimpse of Cousin James and be captivated by his stature and his eyes. Sometimes she would go parading past him flirtatiously and would call out, "Hey, Cousin James!"

He would just laugh at her showing his perfect smile, and she would simply be smitten.

Determined to get James to notice her, she continued for days prettying herself up, changing her hair and switching to outfits that she normally reserved for special company on Sundays. Her daily visits became adventures as she would try different little playful tricks to get James's attention. She would act as if she was helping to water the flowers in the garden and dip her hand into the bucket and sprinkle water on James as he passed by for him to take notice to her. She would giggle apologetically. Her antics began to work as James began to take notice of how beautiful she was with her short hairdos and her tempting taste for dresses and pretty skirts. He liked her outgoing sense of humor and the casual ways she would find to make things around the garden fun to do. James knew that Jane was younger than he was, and this fact alone served as a constant deterrent to him to remember to keep his distance from this young damsel.

But Jane continued her vie for James's attention and affection. One day, her antics got the best of him, and she beckoned him with her finger and then began to run down the lane. For a moment, he wondered if something was wrong because Jane had a serious look in her eyes instead of the typical giggle that he would have normally taken notice of. James looked around to see if she was pointing to someone else, but she was now calling his name. He stopped in his tracks and asked if she was all right, then quickly followed her, as she ran down the lane. It was evening time, and she was headed toward a small but secluded spot. When she stopped running in front of him, she turned and first giggled before she then began to talk to him. They talked for hours. She asked him question after question about himself: Where was he from? Where was he going? Why was he not living there before? Where was his father and other siblings living, and what was his life like at his other home?

James found himself fascinated by this young girl—her smile, her hair, her funny cute ways. He couldn't get over how much interest he had developed in watching her stroll through the garden with his cousin. Jane confided in Martha about the meeting between her and James. Their meetings became more and more regular with Martha acting as the watch out person! They would meet in his mother's barn, the woods behind James's house, and sometimes in Audrey's house while she was away at work. James managed to control himself since Jane was so young. He loved being with her, talking and listening, and she mesmerized him as she would move about playfully and so freely without a care in the world. He would watch her in amazement, wishing that she was not so much younger than he was.

Soon, a forbidden love affair developed between the two of them. He simply could not help himself. She would lean onto his shoulder in their secret meeting spot, and he would reach into his pocket and give her a little money to spend at school. Nothing sexual happened, but they were beginning to fall in love. They both became deeply interested in one another; they loved laughing and spending time together. Sometimes he would buy her a small gift or treat and bring it to their secret meeting place to give it to her. They would sit out under the stars till after dark and listen to each other. Jane would tell James what happened at school or joke about the basketball team losing games, and James would tell her about all the new things that he was learning at work and about the products that his company was making. By now, he was being seen as a leader at work and was asked to be over the other guys. Talking with Jane about work, being with her, and giving her money and small gifts which she kept secret made James feel like a man. Things could have become really hot, heavy, and sensual between them, but then World War II broke out, and James, every able-bodied man, and working-age boy in their hometown was off to the war.

By then, Jane was love struck! James would write her letters and send them through his cousin, Martha, as often as he could write, but after a while, the letters came less often. Jane's love for James did not wane. James was in a foreign country now where he experienced a freedom and women like he had never experienced before. Every now and then, he would think about that sweet funny young girl back home.

World War II kept James away from home for at least three years. As soon as James could return, he hurried home. They would all get together for dancing at the nearby juke joints. The juke joints would be filled with ex-military men, and the young women were just hoping to meet someone to have a good time with, and eventually if they were lucky enough—to marry.

During the war, Jane had grown into a beautiful young woman. At sixteen years old and in her last year of high school, she was now anticipating her first real love. She secretly wished her relationship with James would pick up where they had left off before the war. However, a situation was developing that would change both their lives forever.

Aunt Bertha and Audrey had successfully managed to marry off all of their daughters into good families. But Jane's mother, Ruth, had not been so lucky in marrying off Rosemary, Jane's orphaned cousin. Rosemary had indeed been married off into a good and decent family before the war. Her husband, Steven, went to war leaving her his small savings that he had saved up to start his own building and construction company when and if he returned home alive. It was his dream—that and coming home to his lovely wife. But Rosemary was not faithful. She never followed the wisdom of her aunts, and she spent up all the money her husband had saved. What's worse, it was rumored that Rosemary was in love with another man. It was enough to make her aunt, Ruth, a nervous wreck.

Soon after the war ended and the men came home, Steven divorced Rosemary and set off to reconstruct what he could reconstruct of his life and his small savings. Divorced by her husband, Rosemary was now bent on finding another man to provide for her. She didn't want to disappoint her aunt further by marrying the other man whom her aunt did not approve of. So when her aunt suggested that she pursue James, Rosemary thought he was the perfect suitor to pacify her aunt. Even though Rosemary was secretly in love with the other man, she sat out to catch James, following her aunt's advice. Rosemary was not the least bit interested in James, but she was interested in having his money. Rosemary and her aunt did not know that Jane and James were interested in each other, nor did they know that Jane had fallen in love. Martha and Jane had managed to keep that a well-kept secret before and during the war.

Rosemary had always felt a sense of entitlement because her mother had instilled it in her as a child before her mother died. Of the two girls, Rosemary had been made to feel that she was the prettiest and the most special. Her aunt would always make a fuss over her, commenting about her longer hair and lighter skin complexion. This favoritism had always made Jane feel left out, and it made Rosemary feel that she could have whomever or whatever she chose. Soon Rosemary began to go after James with everything she had, admitting that she did not love him. She appreciated the fact that he had become quite a catch with industrial knowledge he had gained while in the military. He had saved his money and done quite well for himself; he would be a great catch for any young woman, thought Rosemary. And moreover, he was financially independent.

James had always been a resourceful young man. James began making plans to have his first home built from the ground up. Rosemary had already devised a scheme in which she would have her cake and eat it too. She saw the opportunity to marry James to satisfy her aunt and provide for herself a good meal ticket. Not knowing how Jane felt about James, Rosemary would have Jane accompany her and James to the juke joint. Once there, she would tell Jane to keep James company while she went to seek out her lover that her aunt didn't want her to have. Jane was given instruction to get with James and keep him occupied by dancing with him and plying him with liquor. Meanwhile, this would give Rosemary the chance to steal away to her forbidden lover.

James still enjoyed Jane's company. He remembered the days they snuck away together as teens, even though he was years older than she was. James thought that Jane was so much more fun to be with than Rosemary, so when Rosemary left the table, he didn't object because Jane was the one he had always had many great laughs with. Her orphaned cousin would give Jane strict instructions to keep James on the dance floor. And that Jane did! When Rosemary would come back to the table, Jane would speak of how much fun she and James would be having on the dance floor doing a dance called the "Truck." Jane was laughing and having so much fun together with James, but Rosemary did not pay attention! Her motive was to totally have her secret love without her aunt or anyone else finding out. At the same time, the secret love that was birthed between James and Jane was quickly rekindled.

On one of those evenings, James had too much liquor, and he and Jane had too many slow dances together, they slipped outside to his brother Ed's parked car. James began to kiss Jane passionately and fondled her body. Before he knew it, he had done the unthinkable. Jane was so naïve; she thought they were just going to kiss like the short times before in their secret hideaway down the lane. But her naïve responses were no match for the seasoned veteran James had become at making love to women in other countries during his time in the military. Although he never fell in love with any of the women he slept with, James had developed a pattern so much like his dad. He would have to have all of her that evening; he could not keep his mind off of her, and she was a willing young girl in love.

Once they were outside the juke joint, Jane was silly enough to think that James had not missed Rosemary's presence at the table. After they were in the car, he told Jane he noticed, but he really didn't care as long as he could enjoy her company. They never discussed much about Rosemary at all in the car after that. All they wanted to do was get lost in each other. After several hours of love-making, they straightened their clothes and re-entered the juke joint separately.

CHAPTER 6

Jane's Lost Love

Weeks passed and led to a month. Rosemary had practically moved in with James at his mother Audrey's house while his house was being built. Rosemary's aunt was so disappointed that Rosemary was settling to shack up instead of marriage. Her aunt warned Rosemary that she and James would be expelled from the church, and James would be stripped of his position in the Free Masons. To compound matters, James's family did not approve of the relationship between Rosemary and James either. His Aunt Mary would come to Audrey's house packing her big gun folded under her arms when Rosemary was visiting at Audrey's. Aunt Mary thought she could intimidate Rosemary and run her off, but her attempts failed. Rosemary was tenacious as a bulldog, and she was not letting go of this approved meal ticket.

Jane's menses were late, and she was feeling sick. Rosemary came home to visit her aunt and get some fresh clothing when she noticed her cousin was not her usual jovial self as the family's clown. Jane's mother took notice to Jane also and began to question her. Jane burst into tears and blurted out that she was late this month, and felt she was pregnant! Rosemary and Ruth began to preach, cry, and fuss with Jane about her predicament. Shocked and in dismay, Rosemary and Ruth raged on for a while before the calculating mother ordered Rosemary to quit raging and Jane to stop crying. Her mother swore each one of them to secrecy, and that they were never to tell anyone about this. Ruth had made a promise to herself that neither of the girls would end up old matron like herself without a good man to take care of them.

Without taking thought as to whom the father was, Ruth decided she had to find a husband for Jane quickly. Rosemary, trying to keep her aunt's attention off of her own escapades, quickly agreed. They didn't even bother to ask Jane about the boy Jane had sex with. They just assumed that it was some young boy, poor and still in high school without any means. They were not interested in knowing how Jane had been spending her time or who she might be in love with. Jane was never made a priority. The attention had always been on Rosemary. And that's the way things had always been. Ruth had loved Rosemary more than Jane since the day Rosemary came to live with them. There was no way Ruth was going to have Jane embarrass her by having a baby out of wedlock. "Besides," Ruth thought out loud. "All the boys in school here don't have anything."

Ruth quickly surmised a list of possible men suitors in her mind. For a moment, she even mentioned one of James's older brothers. But that was out of the question. Most times, he was not even around town as he had remained in the military long after his brother. And when he was home for a military layover, he never hung around the girls in town. Ed always played the field in other outlying areas, trying to find a big city girl. He always thought he was too good for the girls in this part of the country.

Ruth was standing over the kitchen sink washing dishes when a light bulb went off in her mind. *Bingo!* Ruth thought. That young man down the street, Robert, has just returned from the war, and he will have some money and benefits too!

"We will get you married off to that boy Robert, and Rosemary, you will marry James!"

Jane was shocked. *That was the plan?* Jane thought. How could she do that? She was in love with James, and this was his baby! But how could she tell anyone? What would James think about all this, and how could she ever win out over Rosemary? Rosemary was just like Ruth. Once Rosemary decided to do something, that was it, she would always have her way; that was the way it had been all their lives.

Ruth began to fix supper and surmised how quickly she could have Robert over for supper. She instructed Jane that she had to get Robert to marry her quickly so he would think that this was his baby, and she would not be labeled. Jane was knocked off her feet. She didn't know what to do. She was not even finished with high school yet, she thought. What was she to do? The snare was set, and soon Robert was caught in the snare of marriage.

Jane was the baby of the family, but she was treated like the black sheep. She was born after her siblings were old enough to care for themselves as opposed to her who needed care. Her birth was unexpected and unwelcomed. Her mother let Jane know this by her actions and deeds. She would call Jane's orphaned cousin, Rosemary, the pretty child. Rosemary got the best clothes, the choice food, and her aunt's affection. However, Jane's father compensated for the lack of her mother's affection. Jane's father loved her very much. When he wasn't working, he spent quality time with Jane, taking her places, and showing her things. They were together constantly. Jane was also showered with affection from her aunts and uncles on her mom Ruth's side. That was the only way she was made to feel special and smart.

Ruth's people were landowners with houses, orchards, livestock, and laborers. Jane would roam acres and acres of land with her Uncle Jim. She would observe him weigh his laborers cotton, and he would engage her in simple math problems. Jane was so smart! She would correct her Uncle Jim when he would give one of the lady laborers too much credit for her cotton's weight. Uncle Jim would just laugh at her sharp wit. Jane was very special here.

Jane's entire world changed when her father took his family on a visit to see his mother. His mother lived in another part of Louisiana. When they arrived for the visit, her father's mother did not want her son to leave again, and he gave in to his mother's emotional control. He and his family moved in with his mother and the rest of his siblings. One big happy family it was—or so it was supposed to be.

Jane's father worked hard at logging, but he was a weekend drunk and womanizer. He would blow most of the money he made and would have very little left over to care for his family. His wife Ruth had to go to work to provide stable income for the family. She worked long hard hours in white folks' kitchens and restaurants. She worked from dawn to dusk away from the children. Her children were left in the care of the mother-in-law, Mama Louise, their grandmother. Mama Louise never took a liking to Ruth because Ruth was a dark-skinned woman. People her color were regarded as black and ugly in that part of Louisiana. Mama Louise was so prejudiced that she only accepted and valued light-skinned people and those who had straight hair like herself. She had become somewhat accepting of Ruth's children that had lighter skin, curly hair, and light eyes. Poor Jane did not have either. She looked more like her mother, while Rosemary looked more like her uncle.

Jane and her siblings learned self-hatred after coming to live in their father's world. They secretly called Mama Louise a mean bitch because she led a lot of cruelty in that house. She would refuse to bathe and comb Jane's hair as a little girl because of her hair texture. Jane's little hair was broken off, and her scalp was full of sand due to neglect. Ruth, on the other hand, could not braid hair. For this reason, Jane's father asked a lady in the community to wash and comb his baby's hair. Jane was so happy to have her hair done that she pleaded with the lady (who would become her future mother-in-law) to please put some curls in my hair.

Jane stood there in her room, alone, and remembered how they were beaten with a switch while they laid in bed after their mother left for work. Then Jane was gotten out of bed and stood up on an apple crate to place biscuits upon the boarder's plates. There were other occasions in which she and her siblings were forced to stand and fan their fair-skinned cousin, while their cousin sat in a chair like a princess. Baby Jane, Baby Jane, what a shame! Jane endured this kind of treatment at the hands of many women in her life: her mom, grandmother, aunts—and now, her cousin, Rosemary.

From all of the cruel things her mother and cousin had said and the way she was being treated by them, Jane was consumed with fear about the pregnancy. At age sixteen, still in high school and having no husband, Jane felt, "Here I am once again–the losing one."

Her mother and cousin teamed up on her and scared her to death about telling anyone she was pregnant. She fell against the wall, crying hysterically. Feeling resentment toward everyone, even the baby she was carrying inside of her, she felt her life was being taken! She thought marrying James would be an escape from this place. But now, with her cousin and mother with their claws on him, how could she ever have a chance? Would he even still want her if he knew she was pregnant? Days went by, and Jane became lifeless.

She cried desperately, thinking how much she missed her dad who was away working in the oil fields now. After his mother had taken him over, her dad just seemed to wither away. He drank all the time. Then finally, he just left. He left a message with the neighbor before he hopped a southbound freight train. The message was that he was going to South Louisiana to work in the oil fields. He said that he would send some money when he could until he could return home again. Jane thought to herself for a moment and just cried some more. They left her mother's world and relatives where they were esteemed and celebrated, to come to her father's world where they were barely tolerated! They left a house of their very own where there was plenty, to come to this place where their mother had to leave them and go to work for a penny. Jane had been celebrated by her mother's people, and now she was in this God-forsaken place! She longed for her home of old, a gentler time, an easier time, a more pleasant time when there was plenty and where she was special! Is this just a terrible dream she thought to herself. And now to be pregnant by a man that she loves who is engaged to her cousin! Jane pondered in her mind, *When will I awake from this horrible dream and when will all be normal again?*

Jane's wonder became anger as she thought about losing her James to Rosemary once and for all. After all, Rosemary was the prettier one. And Rosemary was also James's age, so why would he want to marry a girl still in high school? To tell him or not to tell him was the question, Jane asked herself. Would it be James, her, and their child—or no James? She began to think it was better for her to suffer than to humiliate James publicly. By now, everyone in town knew that he and Rosemary were engaged to be married. Rosemary had wasted no time at her aunt's demand to go in for the kill, and she succeeded in getting James to agree to marry her. How she did it so quickly, Jane did not know because since the night they slept together, James had only come in enough distance to Jane to give her a passing hello. This was a mystery to Jane. Why had James not come around since that night?

Rosemary was a person who never played fair with anything. She got the idea that if she sought the help of the local voodoo woman that she would succeed in knabbing James and having him all to herself. So Rosemary was seen walking to the edge of the woods and along the path to Mama Ida's shack. Mama Ida was known for mixing potions and herbs if your period was late or mixing love potions if you wanted that special someone. Rosemary came upon Mama Ida's old weathered shack and entered the rickety old gate into the junk laden yard. She climbed the creeky old steps onto the porch and knocked on the dilapidated door. Mama Ida inquired, "Who's there?" "It's me Mama Ida," Rosemary announced. "Rosemary? Wasn't you here last month? Don't you girls ever learn to keep your legs closed?" scolded Mama Ida. "No Mama Ida I'm not here for that," stated Rosemary. "Then what you here for?" inquired Mama Ida. "There is this special man I like and I just want to make sure he likes me back," stated Rosemary. "You mean James, don't you?" asked Mama Ida. "Yes, mam, how did you know that Mama Ida?" "Child, Mama Ida always know things." You sho goin to need some help cause James is in love with someone else–a young girl." "There is an older woman that likes him too, but she just using his body." "Well I speck I can help you." "Got my money for the job?" Mama Ida inquired. "Yes, mam, here it is," replied Rosemary and she handed the money over into Mama Ida's wrinkled and weathered old hand. Then Mama Ida turned and lumbered off and left the room to enter her kitchen. She walked over to her canning cupboard and pulled out a couple of jars filled with powders, oils, and herbs. She mixed several concoctions together and returned to the room where Rosemary was standing. Mama Ida handed Rosemary the package or hand she came for. She gave Rosemary instructions for each item. "These here herbs put a pinch or two in his food something like Gumbo." "When you bathe rub this oil behind your ears, between your breasts and thighs, then dust some of this powder in the bed." "This should take care of James and any other man you want!" instructed Mama Ida. Rosemary repeated all of the instructions to make sure she had them correct. Then she thanked Mama Ida and bolted out of the door hurriedly. Rosemary couldn't wait to get home and start that pot of Gumbo! She decided to cook at her Aunt Ruth's house so she could cook like she wanted to without being scrutinized. Afterward she would take just enough food home for James to eat. Rosemary got that pot of Gumbo boiling in no time flat and then she went about bathing and making herself beautiful and placing that oil in just the right spots. She smiled inwardly to herself for the plan she and Mama Ida had put in place. Well, after that night Rosemary led James around like a pig with a ring in its nose. James did whatever Rosemary told him. It was a mystery to everyone else including Jane about James's behavior, but it was no mystery to Rosemary. It was just all a part of the game plan. All is fair in love and war!"

As a military man, she began to realize that he had been with women before from different parts of the world. Now to know that her cousin Rosemary was to wed James was a dagger in her heart. Jane knew deep within the crevices of her heart that James really did love her! She now carried his flesh and blood, yet another woman was in line to enjoy a life with James.

Everyone knew Rosemary had been staying with James at his mother, Audrey's, house for a while. Now, Jane began to think it was a noble thing for her to keep the baby a secret rather than smear James's good name.

But how can I pawn this baby off on someone else? she thought. *I would rather die than betray my beloved James*, she concluded. She began to think of ways she could get out of this hell hole away from these two wretches, Ruth and Rosemary.

All they do is take from me! she continued. *Now they have taken my beloved James! Why hadn't James stood up for me?* she wondered. Why hadn't he said anything or been around?

Rosemary was the one going all around town, telling everyone about their wedding. James wasn't saying a thing. Jane had not seen or heard from him at all. "It is as if I don't exist!" said Jane. "Just like it always is with my mother and cousin. They have always acted as if I don't exist," Jane said to herself as she slid to the floor of her room and cried herself to sleep that night. As far as she was concerned, her life was over. She didn't care who she married or what happened to her. Life, as she knew it, was gone.

CHAPTER 7

Who am I?

My mother, Jane, kept her secret, and I was born just five days before Christmas. All my life, I felt like I was the Christmas present she really did not want. I have surmised all of these stories, just so that I can have some peace about who my real father was. Some of these stories were based on fact, and some of them were purely fictitious. It has been many years now, and those who knew the truth—if any—are all gone. Those who are left, if they know, they don't want me to know.

Rosemary and James were married, but they were childless. Rosemary had not yet been able to conceive. James began to shower his affections toward me and helped Jane any way he could. Rosemary even helped with me until she saw that her husband cared too much for me. She knew if she wanted to keep him, she had to have a baby of her very own. Rosemary then encouraged James to move out west, and as destiny would have it, they ended up in the same city that my mother and her husband were living.

Yes, my mother did marry Robert, and for some time they had moved west. But as luck would have it, their marriage was rocky right off the bat. For a short time, she left him and returned to Louisiana until I was born and old enough to travel back. In the meantime, James convinced his great-uncle and wife to stand in place and christen me as his godchild before my mother left Louisiana to return to her husband. So James became my parrain, and Rosemary my marraine! This is a role they never fulfilled, that I am aware of.

My mother returned to her husband after I was several months old. Life was not the same between them. Her husband said it was due to the fact that her orphaned cousin, Rosemary, was living there now; and Rosemary meddled in their affairs. My mother said he was a gambler, excessively jealous, and abusive.

Jane remained married to Robert for about a year before she decided to leave for good, and she returned home to Louisiana to her parents. I then became my grandparents' child, and they showered me with love and affection. God saw fit that I was not left abandoned by the circumstances of my mother and the dad whom I imagine. The gapping wound that I felt growing up has begun to heal through my knowing of the Word of God. In the Bible, there are two scriptures which give me peace in not knowing my real father.

It says in Psalm 27:10, "When my father and my mother forsake me, then the Lord will take me up" (Psalm 27:10, KJV.)

In 2 Corinthians 12:2, it states, "I knew a man in Christ above fourteen years ago, whether in the body, I cannot tell; or whether out of the body, I cannot tell: God knoweth."

One thing I know for sure is that God knows who my father was, and God cares about me. He heard the harsh words that were spoken over me as a child, and He allows me to me write these stories from my imagination to release my frustration, hurt, and pain. The scripture goes on to say about the man in 2 Corinthians 12:4, "He was caught up to paradise. He heard inexpressible things, things that man is not permitted to tell."

For whatever reasons, the people who spoke those harsh words and kept secrets to themselves have not been permitted to tell. When one does not know the truth, one is at the mercy of one's own imagination, and this becomes truth to you! I imagine Dad because that's where the story of my real dad lives—in my imagination.

As countless men and women across the globe search for their father, I pray that God gives us all continued revelation in our quest for the Dad we all imagine.

My saga carries on, as I continue to write the next chapters in the pursuit of Dad, hoping that one day "I imagine Dad" will become "this is my dad!"

About the Author

Frances McHenry is a retired educator born in Lousiana who has spent many years educating and mentoring children. She was a nominee for Teacher of the Year by both the Houston Area Association of Black School Educators and the Houston Hispanic School Educators, as well as a presenter/demonstration teacher and mentor in Houston ISD. She also served as adjunct professor of intensive English at Houston Community College.

Frances spent a brief time as a librarian before becoming a teacher where her passion for books and storytelling was ignited.

After retirement, Frances began writing, and from her manuscripts has come the compelling story *I Imagine Dad.*

She resides in Houston, Texas, with her family where she loves to read, cook, entertain family and friends, travel, decorate, and attend workshops and conferences as a life-long learner.

CPSIA information can be obtained
at www.ICGtesting.com
Printed in the USA
FSOW01n2245101215
14032FS